TREES

Library of Congress Number: 84-26225

Library of Congress Cataloging-in-Publication Data

Kirkpatrick, Rena K.
  Trees.

  (Look at science)
  Includes index.
  Summary: Easy-to-read text and illustrations introduce various kinds of trees.
  1. Trees—Juvenile literature. [1. Trees] I. Title. II. Series.
QK475.8.K57   1985   582.16   84-26225

ISBN 0-8172-2359-2   hardcover library binding

ISBN 0-8114-6905-0   softcover binding

    4 5 6 7 8 9 10   96 95 94 93

TREES

By Rena K. Kirkpatrick
Science Consultant

Illustrated by Jo Worth and Ann Knight

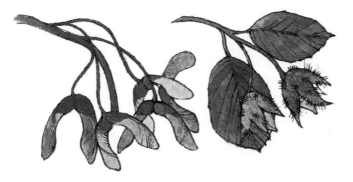

RSVP
RAINTREE
STECK-VAUGHN
PUBLISHERS
The Steck-Vaughn Company

Austin, Texas

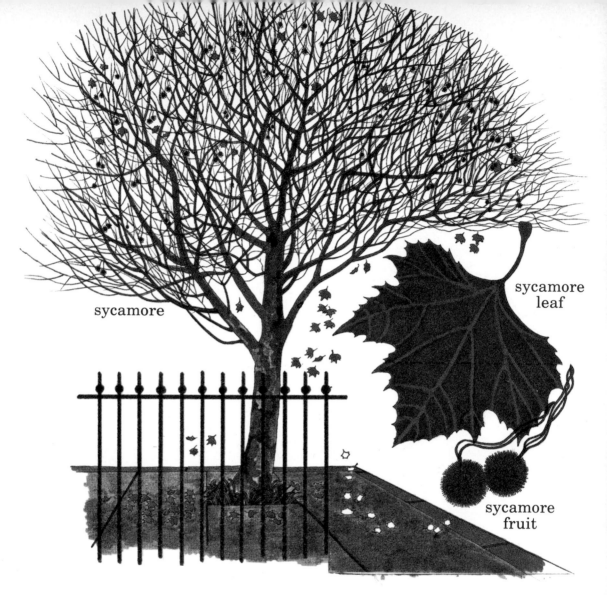

sycamore

sycamore
leaf

sycamore
fruit

What are trees?

Trees are the largest plants in the world. They are used for many things. We get fruit and nuts and medicines from trees. We also get wood. We make paper from wood.

rowanberries

whitebeam berries

cherry

whitebeam

rowan

birch

Where do trees grow?
Trees are planted in parks, in our
yards, and along roads. Trees give us
shade. The leaves and bark and fruit
are colorful. There are thousands of
kinds of trees.

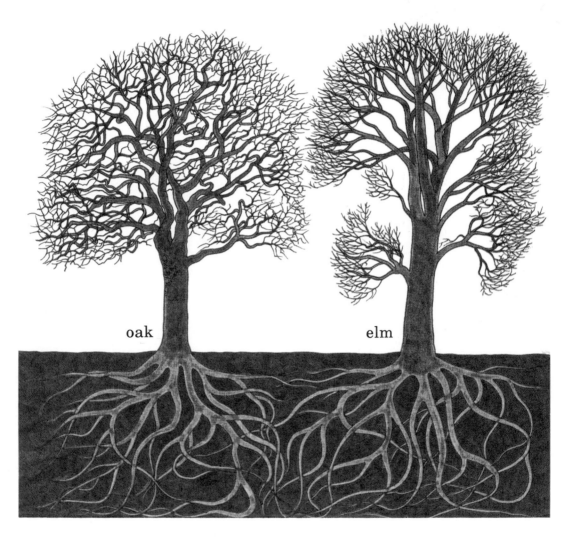

oak

elm

How do trees begin life?
    Trees grow from seeds. As trees get
bigger, they grow roots. The roots
take food and water from the soil.
The roots hold trees up. Some trees
are 200 feet (61 meters) tall.

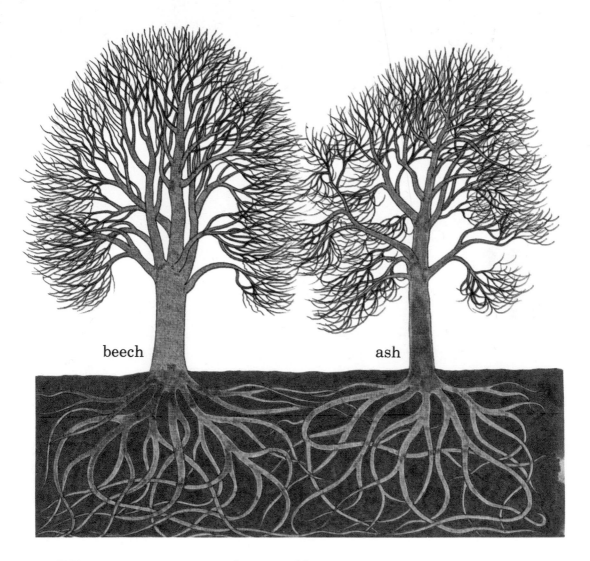

beech

ash

How are trees shaped?
    The branches of each kind of tree
    grow in a special way. All trees have
    different shapes. Birds, squirrels, and
    some other animals build homes in
    trees.

What is a forest?
  We call a place where many trees
  grow close together a forest. In a
  forest, the bottom branches of the
  trees die. That is because sunlight
  cannot reach them.

What happens to trees in the fall?
In places where winter is cold, some
trees lose their leaves in the fall.
They are called deciduous trees.

yew

holly

pine

Do all trees change in the fall?
Some trees have leaves that stay
green all winter. They are called
evergreen trees. Evergreens grow
new leaves before the old ones die.

Scotch pine

dry cone

seeds

Are all evergreen trees the same?
Evergreens that have cones are called
conifers. Seeds grow inside the cones.
When a cone dries, it pops open.
Wind blows the seeds away. New
trees may grow from the seeds.
Conifers have needle-shaped leaves.

larch

flower

Are all conifers the same?
    The larch tree has cones. It is a
    conifer. But the larch loses its leaves
    in fall. It gets new leaves in spring.
    The larch is a deciduous tree.

What are alder and willow trees like?
    Willows and alders grow best where
    the soil is cool and moist. They
    usually grow near water. Both trees
    have flowers called catkins.

How can you tell how tall a tree is?
    Ask a friend to stand by a tree.
    Measure your friend by sighting with
    a stick. The tree in this picture is six
    times taller than the girl.

rings

How can you tell how old a tree is?
Some tall trees are young. Some
small trees are old. A tree's trunk has
rings. A tree grows one ring each
year. If you count the rings, you
know how old the tree is.

What is bark?

The outside of a tree is called bark. It
protects a tree. Bark is like a tree's
skin. You can make a bark rubbing.
Put a piece of paper against the bark.
Then rub a crayon over the paper.

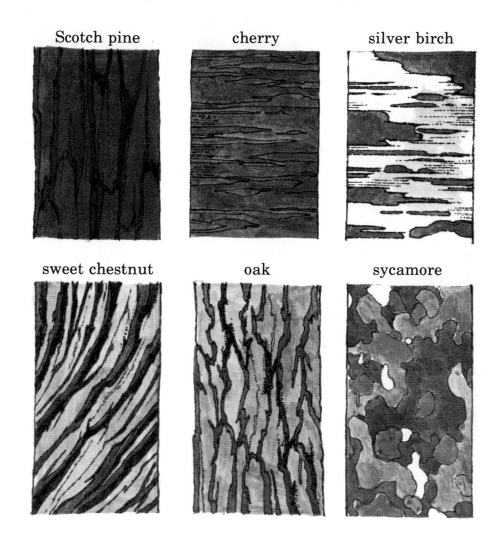

Scotch pine   cherry   silver birch

sweet chestnut   oak   sycamore

How are barks different?
Some trees have very rough bark.
Some trees have smooth bark. Bark is
smooth because it stretches when the
tree grows. Make bark rubbings and
see if they look like any on this page.

How are leaves different?

Some leaves are the size of your fingernail. Some are 20 feet (6 meters) long. In this picture, the pine, holly, and yew leaves stay green all winter. The other leaves drop from the tree in fall.

Why do leaves change color?

Leaves of deciduous trees have many colors in them. In summer something hides the colors and makes leaves look green. But in fall you can see the reds and yellows and other colors of leaves.

Can you make twigs grow?
    In early winter, find some twigs.
    Carefully cut them from the tree. Put
    the twigs in a jar of water. In spring,
    the twigs will grow.

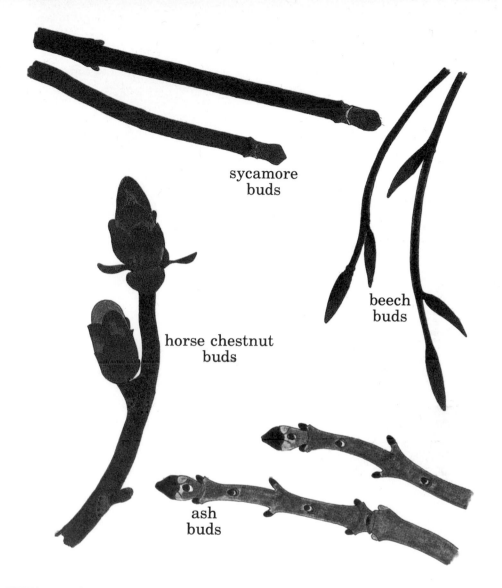

sycamore
buds

beech
buds

horse chestnut
buds

ash
buds

What happens to the buds of trees?
Buds grow on the twigs of trees.
Some buds are green. Some are large
and sticky. Some are black. In spring,
buds become leaves or flowers.

sycamore flowers

apple blossom

rowan flowers

horse chestnut flowers

poplar catkins

What are the flowers of trees like?
All trees have flowers. They look
different from flowers you usually
see. New trees grow from the seeds
in the flowers. Catkins are unusual
flowers.

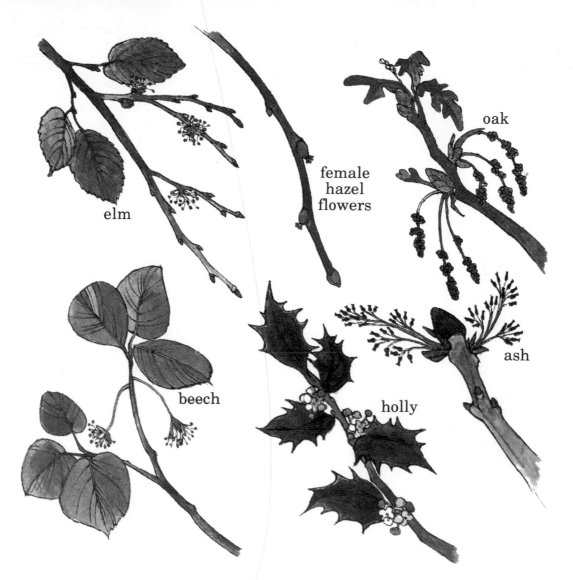

elm

female
hazel
flowers

oak

beech

holly

ash

Which trees have very small flowers?
　　The flowers of these trees are so tiny
　　that they are hard to see. You have to
　　look carefully for them in the spring.
　　They only live for a few days.

What is fruit?

The part of a tree that has seeds is called fruit. Some seeds are big. Others are very small. People eat the fruits of some trees. Fruits are good for you to eat.

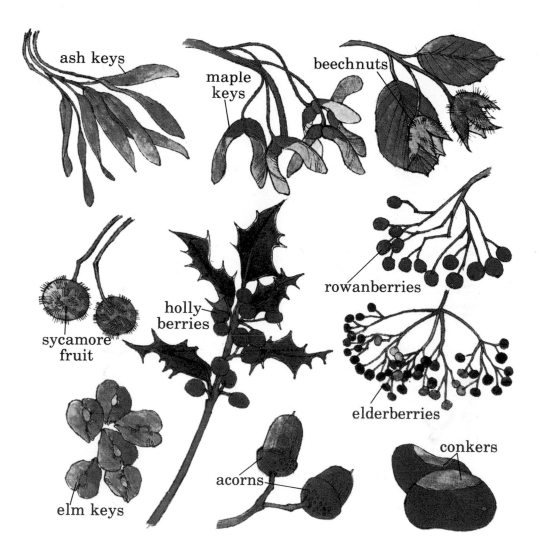

ash keys

maple keys

beechnuts

rowanberries

sycamore fruit

holly berries

elderberries

elm keys

acorns

conkers

Can people eat all fruits?

Most of the fruits in this picture are not good for you to eat. Some taste bad. Some can make you sick. These fruits are good for birds and animals to eat.

Will all seeds grow?

Find some seeds. Then plant them. Keep the soil moist. Some seeds will not grow. Others will grow. It may take many weeks for the seeds to begin to grow.

How do seeds travel?
  Maple seeds spin when they fall.
  Other seeds float in the air. The wind
  blows these seeds to new places.
  Birds and animals also carry seeds to
  other places.

Why are trees useful?
Birds and some animals build their houses in trees. We get wood and paper from trees. How many paper things and wood things can you find in this picture?

Are woods different?

    You know that trees have different shapes and bark and fruits. Wood is different, too. Some wood is as light as paper. Some wood is soft. Some is hard. Each tree has its own beauty and uses.

Look at Trees Again

Trees are the largest plants in the world.

Trees grow from seeds.

There are thousands of kinds of trees.

Roots hold a tree up.

Deciduous trees lose their leaves in fall.

Leaves of deciduous trees change color in fall.

Evergreen trees keep their leaves in winter.

Evergreens that have cones are called conifers.

A tree trunk grows one new ring each year.

Bark protects trees.

Leaves and flowers grow from buds.

People eat the fruits of some trees.

Trees are useful to people and animals.

Look at These Questions About Trees

1. Why do trees need roots?

2. How do trees begin life?

3. What is a forest?

4. What do deciduous trees do in the fall?

5. What kind of tree keeps its leaves in winter?

6. How can you tell how old a tree is?

7. What does bark do?

8. What do the leaves of deciduous trees do in the fall?

9. What grows from tree buds?

10. What part of a tree has seeds?

ANSWERS

1. To hold them up as they grow bigger.
2. They grow from seeds.
3. A place where many trees grow close together.
4. Lose their leaves.
5. Evergreen.
6. By counting the rings.
7. Protects trees.
8. Change color.
9. Leaves or flowers.
10. The fruit.

Words in TREES

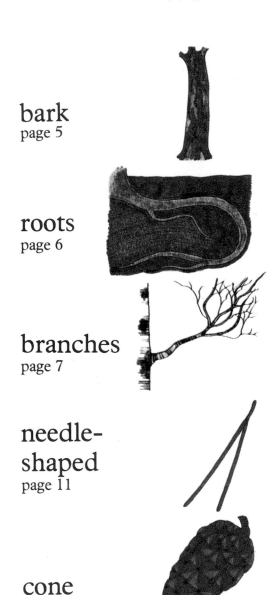

bark
page 5

roots
page 6

branches
page 7

needle-
shaped
page 11

cone
page 11

pussy
willow
page 13

twig
page 20

bud
page 21

catkin
page 22

maple
seeds
page 27